Melissa

Disney PRINCESS

palace pets

Ultimate Handbook

Illustrated by the Disney Storybook Art Team

Random House 🏠 New York

ISBN 978-0-7364-3421-8

randomhousekids.com

Printed in the United States of America

10 9 8 7 6 5 4 3 2 1

Welcome to the world of Palace Pets!

Each of these lucky little animals is a princess's best friend. They wear tiaras, live in castles, and go on exciting adventures. And just like you and your friends, they have their own likes and dislikes.

Turn the page to learn all about the adorable Palace Pets and find out how each one became part of a royal family. . . .

Bayou

Animal type: pony

Color: lemon yellow with a violet mane and tail

Princess pal: Tiana

Did You Know?
Bayou lives in the stables at Charlotte La Bouff's fancy estate.

Berry

Animal type: bunny

Color: fluffy blue

Princess pal: Snow White

Did You Know?

Berry loves to eat blueberries—
that's how she got her name!

Bibbidy

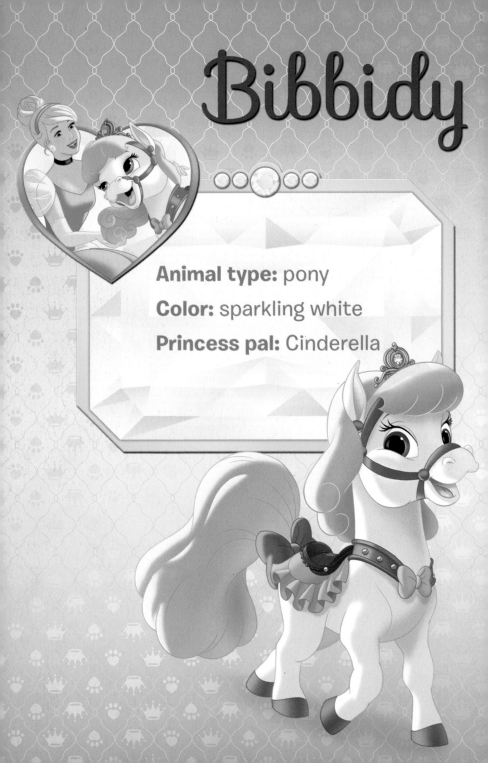

Animal type: pony

Color: sparkling white

Princess pal: Cinderella

Did You Know?
Bibbidy is a very helpful pony.
She enjoys doing chores.

Blondie

Animal type: pony

Color: regal blond

Princess pal: Rapunzel

Did You Know?

Blondie loves to have her long mane brushed and braided.

Bloom

Animal type: pony

Color: lovely pink with a purple mane and tail

Princess pal: Aurora

Did You Know?

Bloom is a natural performer who likes to be the star of every special event at the palace.

Blossom

Animal type: panda

Color: pale periwinkle face and body with dark periwinkle ears, legs, and tail

Princess pal: Mulan

Did You Know?
Blossom is always hungry.
If she were granted one wish,
it would be for snacks!

Daisy

Animal type: puppy

Color: furry yellow

Princess pal: Rapunzel

Did You Know?
Daisy loves to run around
in circles until she gets dizzy.

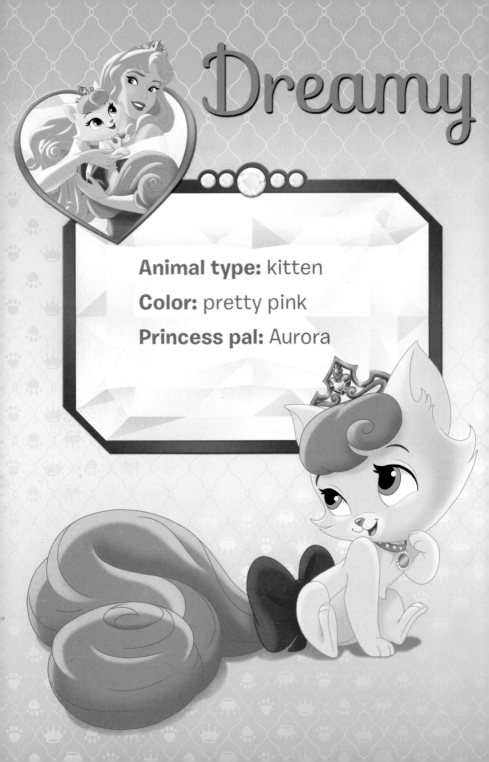

Dreamy

Animal type: kitten

Color: pretty pink

Princess pal: Aurora

Did You Know?
Dreamy loves to nap, especially curled up next to Princess Aurora.

Lily

Animal type: kitten

Color: jazzy lilac

Princess pal: Tiana

Did You Know?
Lily loves jazz music! She dances along to the beat when Louis the alligator performs at Tiana's restaurant.

Matey

Animal type: puppy

Color: perfect purple

Princess pal: Ariel

Did You Know?

Matey doesn't know how to swim. Luckily, he has Princess Ariel to give him lessons.

Meadow

Animal type: skunk

Color: sweet lavender

Princess pal: Rapunzel

Did You Know?
Meadow loves being with people—even though most everyone tries to get away when a skunk comes near!

Petite

Animal type: pony

Color: glamorous gold

Princess pal: Belle

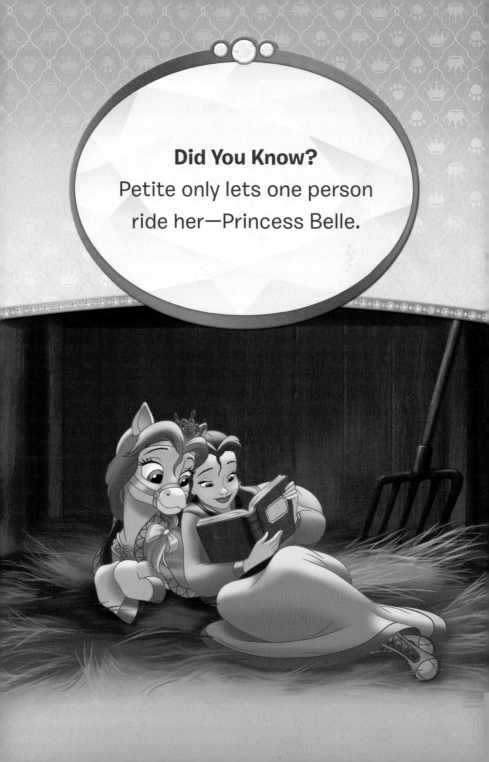

Did You Know?

Petite only lets one person ride her—Princess Belle.

Pumpkin

Animal type: puppy

Color: silky white

Princess pal: Cinderella

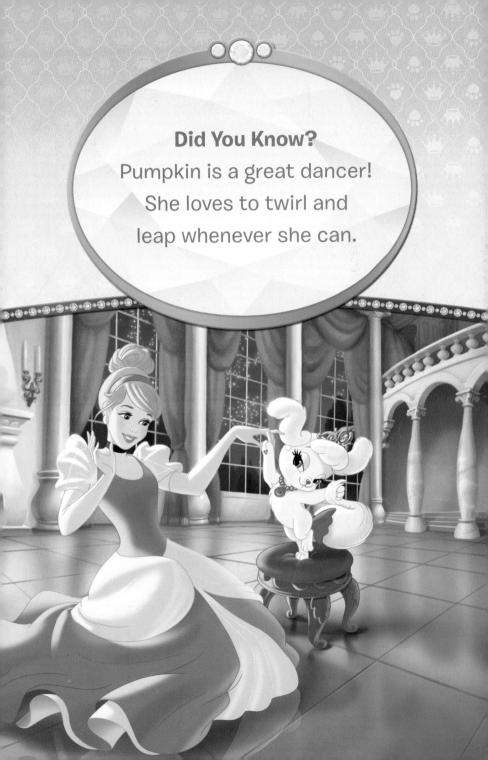

Did You Know?
Pumpkin is a great dancer!
She loves to twirl and
leap whenever she can.

Seashell

Animal type: pony

Color: proud purple with a royal red mane and tail

Princess pal: Ariel

Did You Know?
Seashell used to be a sea horse!
She's still getting used to her
legs and swishy tail, so she's
a bit clumsy at times.

Slipper

Animal type: kitten

Color: cuddly light blue with a pink tail

Princess pal: Cinderella

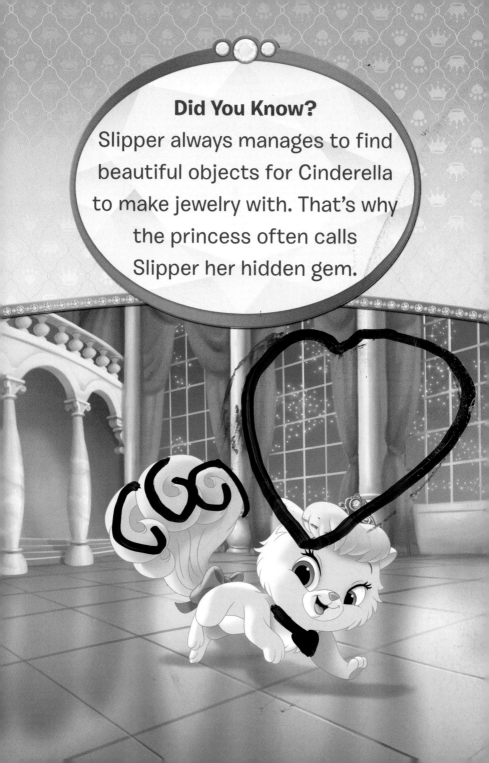

Did You Know?

Slipper always manages to find beautiful objects for Cinderella to make jewelry with. That's why the princess often calls Slipper her hidden gem.

Sultan

Animal type: tiger

Color: awesome orange
with brown stripes

Princess pal: Jasmine

Did You Know?
Sultan is a little tiger, but he is very brave. He will always protect his friends.

Summer

Animal type: kitten

Color: sunny blond

Princess pal: Rapunzel

Did You Know?
Summer loves getting pampered at the Royal Beauty Salon.

Sweetie

Animal type: pony

Color: sky blue

Princess pal: Snow White

Did You Know?

Sweetie loves pie.
This talented pony will dance
for just a taste of one of
Snow White's yummy pies!

Teacup

Animal type: puppy

Color: gorgeous gold

Princess pal: Belle

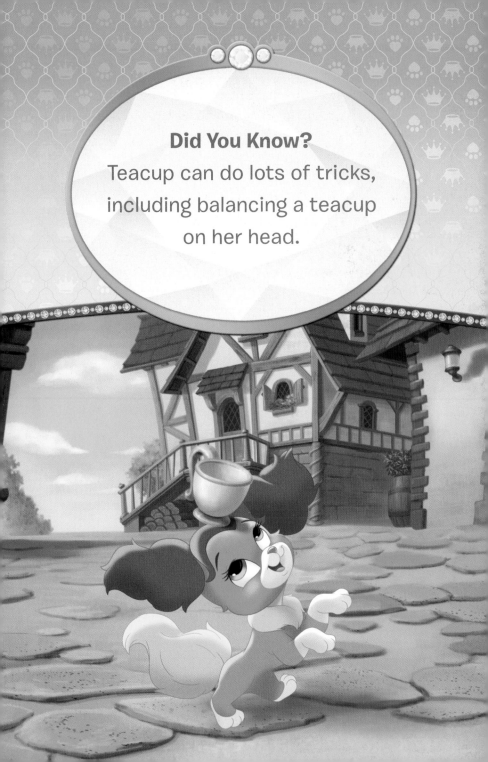

Did You Know?
Teacup can do lots of tricks, including balancing a teacup on her head.

Treasure

Animal type: kitten

Color: coral red

Princess pal: Ariel

Did You Know?

Treasure is a very curious
kitten who loves to swim!

Windflower

Animal type: raccoon

Color: mischievous blue

Princess pal: Pocahontas

Did You Know?
Windflower is a bit of a troublemaker. She likes to have fun and play practical jokes.

Royal Families

How did the Palace Pets meet their princesses? Some were given as gifts. Others were found quite by accident. But no matter how they met, they all are happy to be part of a royal family!

Snow White, Berry, and Sweetie

While she was out one day picking blueberries for a pie, Snow White discovered a shy little bunny in a blueberry bush. The princess offered some of her berries, and Berry hopped out to gobble them up. Berry has been sharing her meals with Snow White ever since!

One day, Snow White was bringing a freshly baked pie to the workers at the royal stable. The sight—and smell—of the pie got Sweetie so excited, she started dancing! The princess was amazed. Now Sweetie and Snow White are best friends.

Rapunzel, Blondie, Summer, Daisy, and Meadow

Blondie was marching alongside the royal horses in a parade once, and she tripped over her long mane. Rapunzel comforted the pretty pony and braided her mane to keep it out of her way. Ever since that day, Blondie has been proud to be Rapunzel's royal pony.

One day, while strolling through the kingdom, Rapunzel found Summer, muddy and alone. The princess took the kitten to the Royal Beauty Salon and got her cleaned up. Now Rapunzel and Summer enjoy going for long walks together.

After Rapunzel and Flynn returned from their honeymoon, the Pub Thugs presented the princess with a special gift— Daisy! This energetic puppy loves to run and run and run. Rapunzel enjoys trying to keep up with her!

Meadow was the first skunk Rapunzel had ever seen. The princess couldn't understand why Flynn was running away from such a cute little creature. She picked Meadow up and fell in love with her. Now this royal skunk lives happily in Rapunzel's castle.

Tiana, Bayou, and Lily

Bayou was a gift from Naveen's family. The prince's parents brought the sweet pony all the way from Maldonia! At first, Bayou was nervous about being in a new place, but she soon fell in love with Tiana—and New Orleans. Bayou and Tiana both enjoy dressing up and performing in the Mardi Gras parade.

One night, Tiana spotted a pretty kitten by her restaurant door. The princess gave Lily some food and was surprised to see her stop eating and happily move her tail along to the jazz music coming from the stage. Now Lily is a regular at Tiana's Palace. She loves to hear Louis play his trumpet every night.

Belle, Teacup, and Petite

Teacup was putting on a show in the village square when Belle first noticed her. The talented puppy was balancing a teacup on her head, until the sun got in her eyes, which made her fall over. Belle invited the puppy to live with her in the palace. Now Teacup is pleased to perform new tricks for her royal best friend.

One cold winter day, Belle found Petite walking near a frozen lake. The princess took the pony home so she could rest and warm up, but then she asked her to stay. Petite is adventurous and likes to explore the palace grounds—but she also likes having a loving friend to come home to!

Cinderella, Pumpkin, Bibbidy, and Slipper

Pumpkin was a surprise anniversary gift from the Prince. While celebrating their first year of marriage, Cinderella stepped out onto the palace balcony and was amazed to see a beautiful dancing puppy! Pumpkin loves living with Cinderella and dancing with her at all the royal balls.

The Fairy Godmother gave Bibbidy to Cinderella as a wedding present. The pretty pony is super helpful. She keeps the royal stables clean and makes sure all goes well at the princess's garden parties.

Slipper hangs out at the royal tailor's shop. One day, when Cinderella broke her pearl necklace, the princess realized how special Slipper is. The clever kitten found the perfect item to fix it with! Now Cinderella makes beautiful jewelry with the one-of-a-kind items Slipper brings to her.

Ariel, Treasure, Seashell, and Matey

Prince Eric spotted Treasure when the curious kitten stowed away on his ship. When Ariel came aboard the next day, she and Treasure immediately knew they would be lifelong friends. They both love spending time on the beach—and in the water!

Seashell used to be a sea horse who dreamed of living on land. Understanding that dream all too well, Ariel knew she had to help. The princess asked her father, King Triton, to use his magic powers to turn Seashell into a pony. Ariel is always there to help Seashell get used to her new legs.

One day, Princess Ariel saw Matey jumping from a boat to the dock. The puppy slipped and fell into the water. Luckily, Ariel was there to rescue him! Matey still can't swim, but Ariel plans to give him lessons until they can safely enjoy the water together.

Aurora, Dreamy, and Bloom

Princess Aurora and the good fairies discovered Dreamy in the palace garden. The pink kitten was fast asleep. Aurora worried that Dreamy might hiss and run off if she woke up and found strangers staring at her. But the sleepy kitten simply leaped into Aurora's arms, purred happily, and fell asleep again.

Bloom was a gift from Prince Phillip. Aurora loves spending time with the talented pony. And Bloom certainly enjoys the attention and compliments she gets from the princess—and anyone else who comes to the palace!

Pocahontas and Windflower

Pocahontas was down at the river when she noticed an old hollow log that seemed to be moving. She peeked inside and found Windflower! The mischievous raccoon had gotten herself stuck while chasing a frog. Pocahontas took her to the village to live. Now she and all the villagers find the adorable raccoon—and the trouble she gets herself into—very entertaining!

Jasmine and Sultan

Jasmine was shopping for fine silks in the marketplace when she accidentally discovered Sultan. The tiny tiger was sleeping under the fabrics! The princess asked the shopkeeper if she could take Sultan home. Now Sultan lives in the palace as Jasmine's royal pet.

Mulan and Blossom

Mulan discovered Blossom at a Moon Festival feast. The hungry panda was hiding under a banquet table, reaching for a snack. Mulan invited Blossom to live with her, and now the princess and the panda share snacks every day!

Who is
your favorite?